FOREWORD

It's a pleasure to know that a new edition of *McDuff Moves In* is available once again for a new generation of readers. Over the years, I have received many letters and inquiries from children, parents, and grandparents about McDuff, some of them asking about the origin of his story.

When I was a child there were many fewer children's books published. This didn't matter much to us. We read the same treasures over and over again. One of my very favorites was Marjorie Flack's "Angus" series. A little black Scottie was the hero of these simple adventures—being lost, being found, being smart, being loved.

If there was an inspiration for the McDuff series it was the Angus books—and our love for terriers. Susan Jeffers and I were both very devoted to our West Highland White terriers. Susan had all the models she needed among our three dogs at the time. I am now on the sixth "Westie" in thirty-five years, Sophie, and she is sixteen years old.

These little terriers are sturdy, hearty, and tough. Westies are loving and clever and bossy as all get-out. I wrote the McDuff books in memory and celebration of terriers.

Lucy and Fred's loving rescue of homeless McDuff adds joy to their lives and shows the beautiful change that kindness and care can make for any homeless dog.

Rosemary Wells

FALL 2019

The Gryphon Press

—a voice for the voiceless—

These books are dedicated to those who foster compassion toward all animals.

© 2019 by The Gryphon Press
First Edition 2019

Text Copyright © 1997 by Rosemary Wells
Art Copyright © 1997 by Susan Jeffers

Text set in Cochin by Bookmobile Design & Digital Publisher Services
Printed in Canada

Library of Congress Cataloging-in-Publication Data
CIP data is on file with the Library of Congress

ISBN: 978-0-940719-42-2

1 3 5 7 9 10 8 6 4 2

I am the voice of the voiceless:
Through me, the dumb shall speak;
Till the deaf world's ear be made to hear
The cry of the wordless weak.

—from a poem by Ella Wheeler Wilcox, early 20th-century poet

McDUFF

MOVES IN

ROSEMARY WELLS · SUSAN JEFFERS

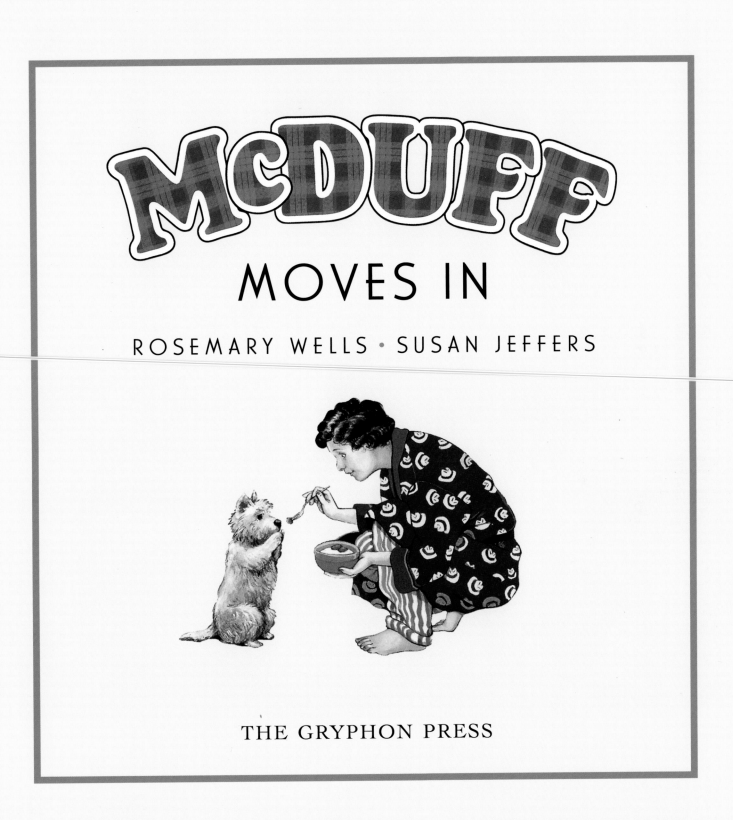

THE GRYPHON PRESS

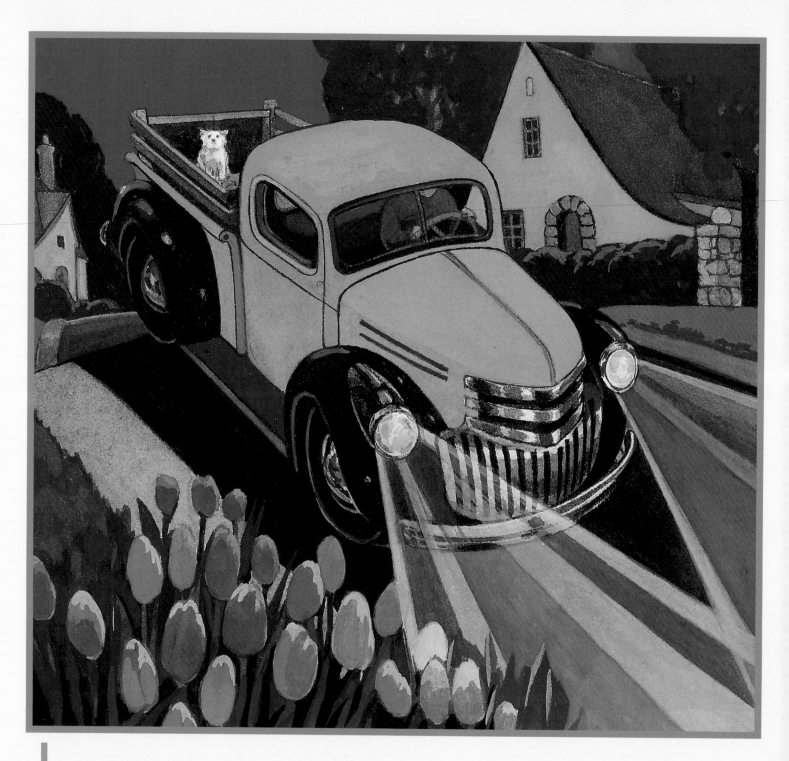

In the back of a dogcatcher's truck
sat a little white dog nobody wanted.

Thump! went the truck over a bump in the road.
The little dog popped out into the night.

He tumbled onto the soft earth of a tulip bed.
He did not know where he was.

He needed something to eat.
He needed a warm place to sleep.
So he went looking.

"Woof!" said the little white dog at the front door
of number six Pine Road. But the answer from
the other side was, *"GROWL!"*

"Woof!" he said on the front steps of number twelve Oak Lane. But someone said, *"Hiss!"* from the woodpile.

Strange voices hooted and whistled at him
from the trees.

Many pairs of eyes winked and blinked at him from
the darkness of people's gardens.

Rain poured down.
It swirled and swept around him.

Suddenly the wind came up.
It blew the clouds and rain away.

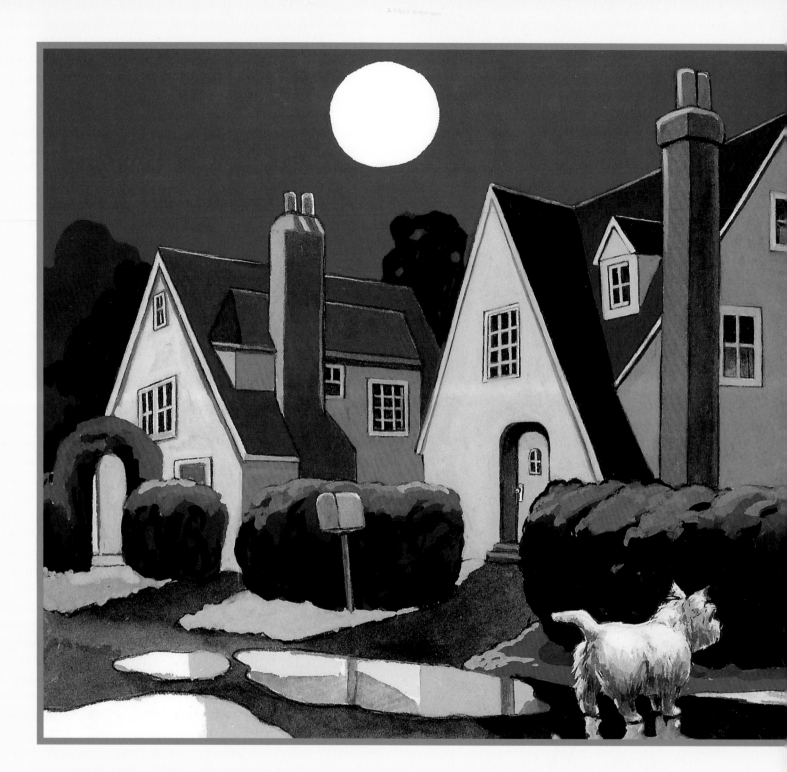

And the moon smiled full on the world. Through an open
window in the kitchen of number seven Elm Road wafted
the smell of vanilla rice pudding and sausages.

"Woof! Woof! Woof!" said the little white dog.

Nobody growled at him. Nobody hissed at him.
Somebody opened the door and asked him to come in.
It was Lucy. "This is Fred," said Lucy.

No one had ever asked him to come in.
Everyone had always told him to go away.

"What does his collar say?" asked Fred.
"Animal number forty-seven . . . city dog pound," said Lucy.
"He needs help," said Fred.

Lucy spooned out a dish of vanilla rice pudding.
She sliced sausages on top of it. "He's hungry," she said.

After a coconut herbal bath he looked like a snow cloud.
"We certainly can't keep him," said Fred.
"We're much too busy."

"I guess we'll have to take him to the dog pound,"
said Lucy. So they brought him into the car.

Fred drove up and down and around.
"You are going in circles, Fred," said Lucy.

"I don't want to find the dog pound," said Fred.
"I don't want you to find it," said Lucy.

Fred and Lucy brought their new friend home.
"All he needs is a name," said Fred.
They celebrated with hot chocolate.

Lucy opened a tin of McDuff's Melt in Your Mouth
Shortbread Biscuits. "That's it!" said Fred.
"Woof! Woof!" said McDuff.

The night was nearly gone.
The rain clattered and spattered over everything.
Lucy and Fred and McDuff fell sound asleep.
"How happy we are!" they said in their dreams.

HELPING A DOG LIKE MCDUFF

In this beloved and vibrant rescue story, giving a stray a good home is a natural and fulfilling act. However, McDuff's story is set in the 1930s, at a time when stray animals were regarded as a public nuisance to be rounded up and sent to the "pound," the community impoundment center. This municipal facility was usually overcrowded, with minimal services for animal care, a place where dogs and cats were disposed of quickly and routinely. At that time, a stray or a lost dog like McDuff would have been very lucky to be rescued and adopted as a family member.

Today, a variety of public and private groups assist lost or strayed animals. Many shelters provide adoption programs, lost-and-found message boards, and other services, as well as including humane education and animal behavior programs. Rescue groups volunteer to work with larger shelters and provide foster homes while sanctuaries offer care for animals considered unadoptable because of health issues. Yet, even with ever-increasing efforts to adopt or rehome healthy animals, the ASPCA estimates that approximately 1.5 million companion animals were euthanized in 2017 in US shelters nationwide.

McDuff's struggle to find a home is repeated many thousands of times every day (see *Cookie's Fortune*). If your family has decided that a dog would make a happy difference in your lives (see *Are You Ready for Me?*), please adopt from a shelter rather than purchasing from a pet store, where animals may be stocked from unhealthy and cruel puppy breeding mills (see *A Home for Dakota*). Consult websites of animal rescue organizations for more information, or search on Petfinder.com, which aggregates available adoptable animals from all over the US and Mexico from nearly 11,000 animal shelters and adoption organizations, with the ability to sort by age, breed, size, and compatibility. Give a dog like McDuff the chance for a happy life and a good home—in your home.

Cookie's Fortune
978-0-940719-39-2

Are You Ready for Me?
978-0-940719-08-8

A Home for Dakota
978-0-940719-36-1